ISBN 0 86112 877 X

This edition first published by Brimax Books Ltd. Newmarket. England 1994.
Printed in France by Pollina, 85400 Luçon - n° 65404

Can I play too?

Freddy Foal is eating in his stable. He is still very young. He has not met the other animals on the farm yet. "Come along Freddy," says his mother, Harriet Horse. "It is time you met all the other young animals on the farm. I am sure you will make lots of friends and have lots of fun."

Harriet Horse leads Freddy out of the stable. The sun is shining brightly. Freddy's long, thin legs are still a bit wobbly. He gallops round the farm making clouds of dust. His hooves are very clumsy still.

"Look, I can see Sally Sheep and her lambs," says Harriet Horse. "Now off you go and play."

Sally Sheep is watching her two lambs, skipping and jumping. Freddy gallops up to them.
"Can I play too?" he asks.
"You are too big to play with us," they say. "You might step on us."
The two lambs start playing together. Poor Freddy is left alone.

Hetty Hen is scratching for corn. Her chicks are playing hide and seek nearby. Freddy gallops up.
"Can I play too?" he asks.
The chicks peep out from their hiding places.
"You are too big to play with us," they say. "You might step on us." The chicks keep on playing. Poor Freddy is left alone.

Gertie Goose is sitting in the sunshine. Her goslings are playing Catch nearby. Freddy gallops up.
"Can I play too?" he asks.
"You are too big to play with us," they say. "You might step on us." The goslings start chasing each other again. Poor Freddy is left alone.

Dilly Duck is waddling across the farmyard. Her ducklings are playing Follow-the-leader. Freddy gallops up.
"Can I play too?" he asks.
"You are too big to play with us," they say. "You might step on us." The ducklings take hold of each other's tails and follow Mrs Duck. Poor Freddy is left alone.

Rosie Rabbit is sitting in the field. Her babies are running in and out of their burrows. Freddy gallops up.
"Can I play too?" he asks. The rabbits stop playing.
"I suppose I am too big to play with you, too," Freddy says sadly. The rabbits nod their heads and pop back into their burrows. Poor Freddy is left alone.

Freddy is in the wood at the far end of the field. The trees are covered in fresh, green leaves. Baby birds have just learned to fly. They flutter between the branches. Young squirrels scamper up and down the tree trunks.

"I know I am too big to play with the birds and the squirrels," says Freddy sadly.

Freddy trots very slowly back to the farm. He feels very sad and lonely. No-one wants to play with him.

"I wish I was not so big," sighs Freddy. "If only the other animals would play with me."

Freddy trots into the farmyard.

He hears the other animals crying. The crying is coming from behind the barn. Behind the barn is a small cart. The lambs, the chicks, the goslings and the ducklings are all sitting inside. They are all crying.

"What a noise!" thinks Freddy.

"Please be quiet," says Sally Sheep.
"They want to ride in the cart," says Hetty Hen.
"No-one can pull it," says Gertie Goose.
"None of us are big enough," says Dilly Duck.
"And I am too big," says Harriet Horse. "But I know who is just the right size."

"Freddy!" calls Harriet Horse.
"All the animals would like to play with you."
"But they said I was too big to play with them," wails Freddy. "I might step on them!"
"Not if they are in the cart and you are pulling it," she says. "Come along. I will help."

Now Freddy is playing with the animals. They are taking it in turns to ride in the cart while Freddy pulls it.
"You are not too big to play with us after all," they all say. "You are just the right size."
Freddy happily agrees.

Say these words again

young	friends
shines	clumsy
gallops	step
might	alone
nearby	places
chasing	again
leader	heads

Who can you see?

Sally Sheep

Freddy Foal

Dilly Duck

Rosie Rabbit

Gertie Goose

Patch learns to bark

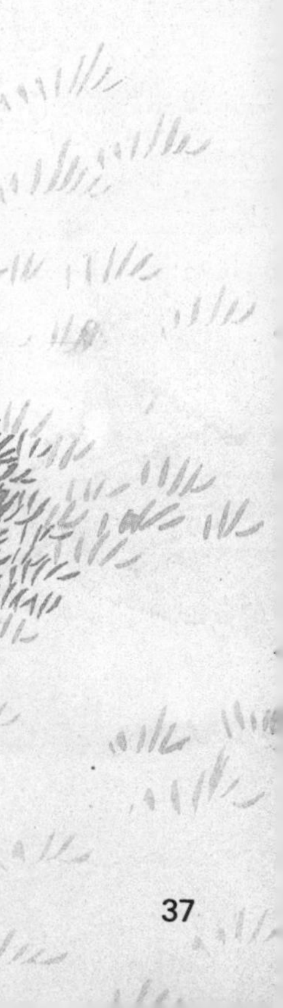

Patch the Puppy lives with his mother, brothers and sisters on Buttercup Farm. Patch can eat his dinner without spilling any. He can wash behind his ears. But there is one thing Patch cannot do. He cannot bark.

"Do not worry," says Mother Dog. "You will learn to bark like the rest of us."
The other puppies are not so kind. "Patch cannot bark," they laugh. "He can only whimper!"

Patch is so upset that he decides to hide until he has learned how to bark. He does not like his brothers and sisters laughing at him.
He creeps over to the barn and sits behind the hay.
There he tries to bark.

"Goodness me!" says Cassie
Calf who lives in the barn.
"What are you doing there,
Patch?"
"I am learning to bark,"
says Patch unhappily.
"I wish I could help you,"
says Cassie. "I can only moo."
"Never mind," says Patch.
He creeps away to find
somewhere else to hide.

Patch does not want anyone
else to listen while he tries
to bark. At last he finds a
dark corner in the hen run.
When the chicks hear Patch
they say to their mother,
“Is there a ghost in the run?”
“No!” says Mother Hen. “It is
only Patch trying to bark.”

"Can you help him, Mother?"
ask the chicks.
"I am afraid not," says
Mother Hen. "I can only
cluck."
Patch tiptoes out of the run
and goes to the pig-pen.

When the piglets see Patch
they all say, “What are you
doing in our pig-pen?”
“I am teaching myself to
bark,” says Patch.
“Can we help Patch to bark?”
the piglets ask their mother.
“I am afraid not,” says Mother
Pig. “We can only grunt.”
Patch goes to the stable.

"What can I do for you?"
asks Dolly Donkey.
"I am teaching myself to
bark," says Patch.
"I would help you if I could,"
says Dolly. "I can only bray.
You will find your bark sooner
or later."
"I have tried very hard and
I still cannot bark," says
Patch.

"I have an idea," says Dolly. "Why not go and practice in the cellar? You might find your bark there," she says. Patch leaves the stable and goes to the cellar. The door is wide open.

Patch goes down the stairs very carefully. He sees a chest lying open at the bottom of the stairs. Patch is very curious. He creeps closer and closer to the chest . . .

Suddenly a frog leaps out
and lands on Patch's nose!
"Woof! Woof!" barks Patch
in surprise. "Woof! Woof!"
He is so scared he runs back
up the stairs. He runs all the
way home to his mother,
barking as he goes.

"Woof! Woof!" barks Patch as he passes Dolly Donkey in her stable.
"Woof! Woof!" barks Patch as he passes the piglets in their pig-pen.
"Woof! Woof!" barks Patch as he passes the chicks in their run.
"Woof! Woof!" barks Patch as he passes Cassie Calf in her barn.

“Is that you, Patch?” calls Mother Dog.
“Woof! Woof!” barks Patch. “I can bark! Something frightened me in the cellar and now I can bark!”
Patch’s brothers and sisters crowd round him.
“I am very proud of you, Patch,” says Mother Dog.
“Woof! Woof!” barks Patch happily.

Say these words again

lives
learn
creeps
hide
corner
afraid
sooner

behind
laugh
somewhere
anyone
trying
teaching
curious

Who can you see?

Patch

Cassie Calf

Mother Hen

Mother Dog

Dolly Donkey

Sam the sheep-dog

Sam the sheep-dog is trying to herd the sheep into their pen. But they will not go in! Five sheep are in the wheelbarrow. Three sheep are asleep in the hay. All the others are playing games in the field. There are no sheep in the pen. "I am not a very good sheep-dog," says Sam.

The next day, Sam wakes early.
“It is the Sheep Show today,”
he says to Dolly Donkey. “All
the sheep must have a bath.
They might win a prize.”
The big bath-tub is filled
with soapy water. Sam goes
to fetch the sheep from the
field.
“I will help,” says Dolly.

But the sheep will not go near the bath-tub.
"Please go in the water," says Sam. But the sheep go in the pig-pen instead. They roll in the mud with the pigs and soon their white coats are very dirty.
"Oh dear," says Sam. "I am not a very good sheep-dog."
"I will also help to herd the sheep," says Curly Piglet.

The sheep run away! They do not go near the big bath-tub. They go inside the hen-house and sit in the straw with the hens.

"Oh dear," says Sam. "Now they have straw and mud on them. They will never be clean for the Sheep Show."

"I will help you to herd the sheep," says Cassie Calf.

But the sheep still will not go into the bath-tub. They go out of the hen-house and past the pig-pen. They go across to the duck pond and splash in the muddy water. Now they are even dirtier!

“Please climb into the bath-tub,” says Cassie Calf. But the sheep go out of the farmyard and across the fields. They wave to the scarecrow and go through the gate. They go down the lane and soon come to the park.

"This looks fun," say the sheep. They climb to the top of the slide and slide all the way down. Then they play on the swings.

"We must go home now," says Sam. "It is nearly time for the Sheep Show." But the sheep are having too much fun.

They play tennis and have a ride on a little train. They have an ice-cream, but it melts and sticks to them. They play in the sandbox and the sand sticks to them as well. “Oh dear,” says Sam. “They have mud, straw, ice-cream and sand stuck to them!”

"We must go home," says Sam. The sheep run past the slide and the swings. They wave to the little train and trot through the sandbox. They run across the grass and into a fountain!
"Oh dear," says Sam. "I am not a very good sheep-dog."

The sheep stand under the cool water.
"They are having a shower," says Cassie Calf. The mud, straw, ice-cream and sand is soon washed away. The sheep are clean and white once more.
"Now we do not need a bath," they say. They walk home to the farm. On the way they see the Sheep Show, they go inside.

There are black sheep with big horns, white sheep with black faces, big sheep and little sheep. There are happy sheep, sad sheep, fat sheep and thin sheep. But the judge gives first prize to Sam's sheep for being the cleanest. They are all given red ribbons and Sam is given a big silver cup.

They walk home feeling very happy.
"Where have you been?" asks Tommy the Cat. "The bath water is cold and you have missed the Sheep Show."
"No we have not," says Sam. "The sheep won first prize!"
The clean, white, fluffy sheep smile. "We had a lovely day out as well," they say.

Everyone is happy. Sam is given a big, juicy bone for dinner. The sheep wear their ribbons all the time and Sam keeps the big silver cup by his bed.

“We think you are a very good sheep-dog, after all,” says Cassie Calf.

“So do I,” says Sam, licking his bone. “So do I!”

Say these words again

herd
wakes
roll
clean
slide
melts
sticks

asleep
soapy
dirty
climb
having
play
stand